The Rose Parade Mystery

THE BOBBSEY TWINS®

THE
ROSE PARADE
MYSTERY

Laura Lee Hope

Illustrated by Ruth Sanderson

WANDERER BOOKS
Published by
Simon & Schuster, New York

Manufactured in the United States of America
10 9 8 7 6 5 4 3 2 1

WANDERER and colophon are trademarks of Simon & Schuster

THE BOBBSEY TWINS is a trademark of Stratemeyer Syndicate,
registered in the United States Patent and Trademark Office

Library of Congress Cataloging in Publication Data
Hope, Laura Lee.
The Rose Parade mystery
(The Bobbsey Twins; 5)
Summary: The Bobbsey Twins search to find the
culprit who is sabotaging the floats for the famous
Rose Parade in Pasadena, California.
[1. Mystery and detective stories. 2. Tourna-
ment of Roses (Pasadena, Calif.)—Fiction]
3. Pasadena (Calif.)—Festivals, etc.—Fiction]
I. Sanderson, Ruth, ill. II. Title. III. Series:
Hope, Laura Lee. Bobbsey twins (1980–   ); 5.
P27.H772Ro   [Fic]   81-11575
ISBN 0-671-43372-5   AACR2
ISBN 0-671-43371-7 (pbk.)

Contents

The author gratefully acknowledges
the Pasadena Tournament of Roses Association
for its kind assistance in the preparation of this story.

The Rose Parade is a service mark
owned and registered,
both federally and in the state of California,
by the Pasadena Tournament of Roses Association, Inc.,
who has kindly given its consent
to our use of the phrase.
Wherever it appears within this book,
it is in reference to an activity
of the Tournament of Roses Association.

· 1 ·

A Ducky Puzzle

"Happy New Year!" exclaimed Flossie Bobbsey to the smiling woman who had just opened the front door of her house.

Six-year-old Flossie belonged to one of the two sets of twins in the Bobbsey family.

"It isn't New Year's Day yet!" Her twin Freddie frowned back.

"But it will be soon!" the little girl persisted.

"And you know what?" Mrs. Hamlin said, wrinkling the freckles across her nose. "By New Year's Day, you'll all solve a mystery!"

"A mystery!" twelve-year-old Nan and Bert cried excitedly.

"We Bobbseys love mysteries!" Freddie declared. He and Flossie whispered and giggled while Nan looked quietly puzzled.

"Mrs. Hamlin, how can you be so sure?" the girl detective asked.

"Let's just say it's a feeling."

"Or a hunch," Bert said. Like his twin Nan, Bert had dark hair and brown eyes. The younger children had blond hair and blue eyes.

"Exactly," Mrs. Hamlin replied, "and speaking of hunches, did Mr. Hamlin say he was going to the float factory after he dropped you off?"

Nan suddenly put her hand to her mouth. "Oh, I forgot—he asked me to tell you he'd be back in a minute."

"It was nice of him to pick us up at the airport," Bert put in. "That way Mom and Dad could catch an earlier plane to Hawaii."

At the mention of it, Mrs. Hamlin gazed thoughtfully through a front window that looked out on a dazzling orange tree.

"Hawaii is beautiful but we still prefer good old Southern California. Pasadena, in particular." She grinned. "Of course, if I were going on a second honeymoon like your parents, I'd probably pick some romantic island too."

Now running footsteps and the entrance of a small, dark-haired boy suddenly stopped the conversation.

"Hi!" he said, breaking into a gigantic grin. "I'm Timmy."

"And I'm Freddie. This is Floss—"

"Want to play with me?" Timmy asked Freddie, ignoring everybody else. "I got a new electric train set for Christmas."

"I *love* electric trains!" Freddie exclaimed.

"Me, too," Flossie said, but the boys paid no attention to her.

Freddie skipped after his new friend, leaving his sister all alone in the hallway while Nan and Bert helped Mrs. Hamlin carry their suitcases upstairs.

Freddie only cares about that dumb train and Timmy, Flossie thought as she walked toward the living room.

There on the carpet stood a narrow silver

track that ran through small tunnels and over tiny mountains. The train itself had a smokestack from which little puffs of smoke rose slowly in the living room air.

"Woo-oo-h, woo-oo-h!" the train whistle sounded as the chain of cars entered the toy tunnel.

"See, this switch can make the train change tracks," Timmy explained to Freddie while Flossie leaned unhappily against the doorway. "It can even go through the town and pick up the mail car. Then it can go back over the mountains and through the tunnels again."

"That's fantastic!" Freddie declared. "It's a lot bigger than the electric train set we have at home in Lakeport. Who gave it to you?"

"Amy Potter," Timmy answered.

"Oh, she's the lady who writes all those books for kids," Freddie said, clearly impressed. "I like her books a lot, especially *Terry and His Magic Pan*."

Now the toy train chugged into the small town and Timmy made it stop by the brown mail car.

"Want to make it pick up the mail car and head back to the tunnel?" Timmy asked.

"Oh, boy, would I!" his curly-haired play-mate replied.

Instantly, Freddie crawled toward the set of switches where Timmy was seated.

"Can I play too?" Flossie asked anxiously.

Without waiting for an answer, she darted toward the train but tripped and fell head-long into the middle of the miniature toy town! The track slid sideways toward the couch and the train flipped over on the carpet.

"Flossie!" Freddie shouted. "Look at the mess you made!"

"I'm sorry," Flossie murmured, slowly pulling herself to her feet.

With tears flowing down her cheeks, she ran out of the living room and into Timmy's father who was just crossing the hallway. He sized up the situation quickly.

"No harm done," he said, throwing his arms around the little girl. He swung her off the floor and tossed her almost to the ceiling! Flossie squealed in delight.

"My, you are getting big," Mr. Hamlin

said as he put the giggling girl down. "I won't be able to do that much longer."

Forgetting about the train, Timmy and Freddie raced toward Mr. Hamlin. The two older twins and Mrs. Hamlin joined them.

"I have a big surprise for all you kids," Timmy's father declared mysteriously.

"What is it? What is it?" Freddie asked.

"I can't tell you just yet—"

"Oh, boy. That makes two mysteries!" Freddie exclaimed, then told about Mrs. Hamlin's amazing hunch.

"Well, before you start investigating anything," Mr. Hamlin said, "how about a visit to my float factory? In a few more days the floats will be ready for the Rose Parade."

"May we help decorate them?" Nan inquired eagerly.

"You bet!"

As everyone headed for the Hamlins' station wagon, Freddie noticed a colorful object hanging from the limb of the orange tree.

"What's that?" he asked.

"It looks just like a toy donkey," Nan observed.

"It's a piñata!" Timmy explained.

"A pizza—what?" Flossie asked.

"Not pizza, dear. Piñata," Mr. Hamlin said. "In Spanish-speaking countries, a piñata is hung from tree limbs or ceilings during holidays, especially Christmas and birthdays. Children of the family take turns trying to break it open."

"There are plenty of surprises inside," Mrs. Hamlin added.

"Like candy and fruit and small presents," Timmy said.

"Do piñatas always look like donkeys?" Bert asked.

"Uh-uh," Mr. Hamlin said. "They come in all shapes and sizes."

"Look, there's a tag on it!" Nan observed, running forward. "It says, 'For Young Detectives Only.'"

"That's us," Freddie said, immensely happy. "Pasadena sure is full of mysteries. It's a good thing we're here!"

"May I break it?" Flossie asked,

"You surely may," Mrs. Hamlin said, tilting her face toward the paper donkey. "But you'll have to put on a blindfold first."

"A blindfold?" Freddie repeated as Timmy's mother darted into the house.

Mr. Hamlin nodded. "That's right," he said, with a glance at the tree. "Son, please give Flossie that long stick over there."

As Timmy handed it to the young twin, Mrs. Hamlin returned with a piece of white cloth. She tied it securely around the little girl's head.

"Turn around once, turn around twice," Mr. Hamlin said. He spun Flossie in place causing her to giggle. "Turn around three times. Now go ahead, dear. Try to break the piñata."

"But I can't see where it is," she wailed.

"Just swing," Nan suggested.

"Yeah, but don't hit us!" Bert quickly added, stepping out of Flossie's range.

"I won't," she replied and swung the stick loosely from side to side.

She took a few steps forward, then raised it high and lowered it on the toy donkey! The piñata broke open, spilling out a shower of newspaper that covered the grass.

"Hooray!" everyone shouted and clapped their hands, while Flossie dropped the stick.

She tore off the blindfold. "Oh, look!" she cried.

A white scroll tied with a big, red bow lay on top of the paper. She dived for it and quickly untied the ribbon. Bert helped her open the scroll.

"What does it say?" Freddie asked impatiently, as his brother gaped at the message.

Nan read it aloud:

IF YOU FOLLOW MY CLUES—
AND PUT THEM TOGETHER—
YOU'LL QUICKLY DISCOVER
MUCH MORE THAN THIS FEATHER!

She displayed the message for everyone to see. "There's a white duck's feather attached," she said excitedly.

"Hmm." Bert scratched his head. "Looks like your hunch about a mystery was right, Mrs. Hamlin."

The woman's eyes sparkled happily. "Now you'd better all get going," she said, urging them into the car.

"But what about all this newspaper?" Nan replied. She picked up several wads.

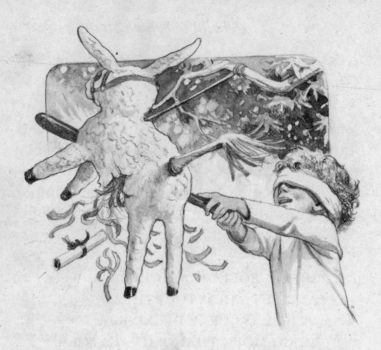

"Thank you, dear," Mrs. Hamlin said, taking them from her. "Just leave the rest. I'll clean everything up. It's more important that you go to the factory and start decorating."

But almost as soon as Mr. Hamlin pulled into the parking lot, a young woman with reddish hair darted toward him. She was obviously upset.

"What's wrong, Mary?" the factory owner asked.

"Come see for yourself. It's terrible, just

terrible. We'll never be able to enter the Honey Bunny float in the parade!"

Without another word, Mr. Hamlin and the children followed the woman to a blue-and-green striped tent that was pitched behind the factory. Inside there were long tables covered with flowers. Many of them were yellow but most were a sickly green!

"Someone poured green dye over them!" Mr. Hamlin exclaimed in despair.

"But who?" Bert asked immediately.

Mary shook her head. "All I know is that the bed of the float has to be draped in yellow. Green flowers just won't do. We'll never be able to replace all of these."

Nan gazed at the long-faced workers who stood sadly by tables filled with useless flowers.

"I have an idea!" the girl detective said suddenly.

·2·

Sprinkled Clues

"What is your idea, Nan?" Mr. Hamlin asked.

"Since you need the color yellow, why not use yellow fruit and vegetables?" the dark-haired girl said.

"That's a super suggestion!" Bert exclaimed. "There must be lots of grapefruit and bananas in California."

"And squash—and what else is yellow?" Flossie asked.

"Lemons!" Freddie shouted.

"And wax beans," Timmy Hamlin added.

"Ugh!" Flossie wrinkled her nose. "I don't like wax beans."

"You don't have to *eat* them, Floss,"

Freddie pointed out. "They're only for the float—"

"We'd better hurry to the grocery story," Timmy broke in.

"Don't get carried away, son," Mr. Hamlin interrupted. "It was a good idea, Nan, but parade officials are very strict about what we may and may not use to decorate the floats."

"Some fruit is permissible," Mary Cleary said.

"Seeds, bark, and leaves, too," another worker added.

"But we're supposed to use flowers mainly," Mr. Hamlin declared.

"Can't Honey Bunny be different?" Flossie asked.

"After all, bunnies like to get into people's gardens and eat vegetables," Freddie said, causing everyone to laugh.

"I'm afraid there are no exceptions to the rules of the Rose Parade," Mr. Hamlin replied.

As he spoke, Bert picked up one of the green blossoms and wiped his finger across it. "I'm sure the dye could be washed off," he observed. "Look!"

Sure enough, the boy had managed to remove a little bit of it just by rubbing. Instantly, Mr. Hamlin and Mary Cleary reached for flowers and wiped them off too.

"You're right!" Timmy's father said.

"Hooray!" Freddie shouted.

"Everyone will have to work fast to save as many flowers as we can," Nan said.

Mary Cleary turned to one of the volunteers. "See if any of the other floats can spare workers for an hour or two."

"Good idea," Mr. Hamlin said.

"Whoever poured the dye on the flowers apparently didn't have time to ruin all of them," Bert said, noting the trail of green color down the center of each table.

One by one, Nan picked the green flowers off the top layer of blossoms. "Oh, look!" she cried happily. "The flowers underneath hardly have any dye on them."

Everyone quickly began weeding out the green flowers.

"The question is, who's responsible?" Bert asked.

"Did any of you see anything suspicious?" Mr. Hamlin asked the float workers.

They all shook their heads no.

"Let's look for clues," Freddie suggested. "Come on, Timmy."

"I'm coming, too," Flossie cried, running after the two boys.

Nan and Bert searched the tent near the tables. In the back were stacks of plywood, some of which had been cut to serve as the frame or "bed" for the float. On one side of the tent were small piles of Styrofoam. The rest of it had been carved into shapes that stood on the float's platform waiting to be covered with hundreds of flowers.

Flossie, Freddie, and Timmy had disappeared into the factory. There they poked into boxes and peered underneath tables, but they could not find any clues.

"What's that?" Flossie exclaimed, pointing to a pair of tall Styrofoam ears in a corner. "It looks like the head of a giant rabbit!"

"That's exactly what it is," said Mary Cleary as she joined them.

"Where's the body? It's not broken, is it?" the little girl asked anxiously.

"Oh, no. It's not broken. It just isn't finished yet," the woman explained. "Small models of each float are made first. Later they are used as guides for the actual, much larger, figures. It takes a while for everything to be built properly."

Timmy walked over to the rabbit head which was half as tall as he was. He picked it up by its long ears.

"It's very light!" he said, rather surprised.

Flossie darted forward and slipped her head into the hollow frame.

"Flossie's the Honey Bunny!" Freddie giggled as she hopped up and down.

"Where's your cottontail, Miss Honey Bunny?" Timmy asked, laughing too.

In reply, Flossie took a giant leap and bumped into a tall stack of boxes!

"Look out!" Freddie cried.

But it was too late! Flossie tumbled to the floor and the boxes fell. They crashed against a large, rusty watering can that hung on a nearby hook. The watering can tipped over, too, sprinkling green water everywhere!

"Help! Help me!" Flossie cried. "I can't get the bunny head off and I'm getting all wet!"

Freddie, Timmy, and Miss Cleary ran to Flossie, pushing the boxes out of the way. They pulled her up quickly and removed the rabbit head.

"Did you hurt yourself?" the woman asked Flossie, checking for cuts or bruises. Flossie shook her head.

Alerted by the noise, Nan and Bert ran into the factory.

"Green water!" they both exclaimed. Bert dashed to the watering can.

"It's a real clue," Nan said.

"That's probably what the vandal used to ruin our beautiful flowers," Mary Cleary said.

"Mixing the dye and the water in the watering can would mean he could cover a lot of flowers at once," Bert said.

"Of course! He simply ran along each table, sprinkling the flowers as he went!" Nan exclaimed.

"So it only took him a few minutes at most to do all this damage," Mary Cleary put in.

Bert studied the hook where the sprinkler had been hanging. "Does this watering can belong here?" he asked the float worker.

"Yes. We have several in the tent where the flowers are kept. This is an extra."

"Then whoever ruined the flowers must have known where to find the watering can," Nan said. "Maybe he used to help decorate floats."

"Anyhow, he was tall enough to hang the can up on the hook," Bert said.

"I can't reach that high," Freddie said as he tried to touch it.

Nan turned to Mary Cleary. "When you arrived this morning, were the flowers all right?" she asked.

"Oh, yes," the young woman said. "When I come in each day, I unlock the factory and go through the tents to make sure everything is just the way we left it the night before. Today after I checked the flowers, I went to the office near the factory entrance to make some telephone calls."

"Then it must have happened while you were on the phone," Flossie exclaimed.

"Someone sneaked in without you seeing him," Nan said.

"But who?" Timmy asked.

"That's what we have to find out," Freddie said.

At that moment, another young woman came into the factory. "Mary, a new group of volunteers has just arrived."

"I'll be right there. I think that they

should begin cleaning and attaching the flowers to the Honey Bunny float," Miss Cleary said.

Nan followed the woman back to the tent while Bert and the other children began to pick up the boxes.

Suddenly, before they were half finished, a loud noise startled them! It was quickly followed by cries of alarm. "Help! Someone help! Come quick!"

They ran outside the building.

"Oh, no!" Flossie cried in dismay.

The tent had collapsed! The blue-and-green striped canvas bobbed up and down as people tried to escape.

Bert's eyes instantly darted to a boy with thick, curly blond hair. He ran around the corner of the building.

As Bert hurried after him, the mysterious boy jumped on a moped hidden in the bushes. He started it, glanced back suspiciously, and sped away from the factory.

Bert raced after the escaping boy!

Honey Bunny Mischief

Bert bolted down the street after the speeding moped. The rider looked back at Bert and began going even faster. Gradually, the moped pulled fully away from the running boy and disappeared around the corner in a cloud of smoke.

Bert stood looking after the mysterious boy for a moment. Then he trotted back to the float factory.

Mr. Hamlin and some of the workers were removing the striped canvas. Bert grabbed hold of one end and helped slide it off one of the long tables. Nan poked her head out from underneath the table.

"Nan!" Bert exclaimed. "Are you all right?" he added anxiously.

His twin got to her feet and brushed her clothing off. "Yes, I'm fine." She laughed. "Fortunately, the tent canvas is fairly light so no one was hurt. We all had time to duck under the tables. But look!" She pointed to the table that had protected her.

The flowers that had been arranged so neatly on it were scattered everywhere. Some of them had been crushed under the pressure of the tent.

As more workers emerged from underneath the canvas, the damaged flowers were gradually sorted out. Mr. Hamlin and three other men raised the tent once again. This time they anchored the sides firmly with cast-iron weights.

"There," Timmy's father said as he drove the last peg into the ground. "We'll post a watch to make sure this sort of thing doesn't happen again. We were lucky no one was hurt this time."

"Just wait till I catch that kid," Bert said.

"Which kid?" Nan asked as she picked up two buckets that had been knocked over.

"Was he the one who tried to make the flowers green?" Freddie questioned.

"I don't know, but I saw a boy take off on a moped right after the tent fell." Bert pointed down the road. "He went along Mountain Street and then onto Fair Oaks Avenue. It looked as if he were heading for Colorado Boulevard."

"That's the parade route," Mr. Hamlin commented.

"Maybe that's another clue," Nan suggested. "What did the boy look like?"

"I couldn't get a full view of his face, but he had blond hair, very curly, and was as skinny as a pencil," Bert replied. "He had on a red plaid shirt and a blue down vest. It was thicker than his whole body!"

"Perhaps it is the same boy who's been making all those phone calls to the Tournament of Roses office," Mr. Hamlin said.

"What does he want?" Flossie asked.

"Well, he *wanted* to ride one of the floats. But he wasn't allowed to. So he's been calling ever since, threatening to cause all sorts of trouble. I didn't connect him with ours until Bert said he saw a boy hanging around here."

"Who is he?" Freddie asked.

The man shrugged. "He never did give his name. Of course, I wouldn't expect him to. Probably just a local boy."

"We ought to hunt for him right away!" Freddie urged.

"I'd love to, but there's no point," Mr. Hamlin said. "Colorado Boulevard is a main street. It's loaded with stores and he could be in any one of them."

"Then maybe we could look for the moped. It might be parked somewhere," Flossie suggested.

"Mopeds are pretty common out here," Mary Cleary added, chucking the little girl's chin. "I think we'll have to track him down later. Right now, we'd better tackle the float."

While they were talking, the volunteers had managed to repair most of the damage caused by the falling tent. Inside the factory, other workers stretched chicken wire over the float's wooden frame.

"What are they doing that for?" Flossie asked.

"That's where the flowers will be set," Mary explained. "Do you see the colors painted on the frame? They indicate the color of the flowers that will be used."

"The chicken wire," Mr. Hamlin continued, "will be sprayed with a polyvinyl material to provide a surface to glue the flowers on. That process is called 'cocooning.' "

"Oh, goody," Freddie cried. "Butterflies!"

Mr. Hamlin tossed his head back in laughter. "There won't be any butterflies coming out of this cocoon," he said, "but there will be a bee. C'mon, I'll show you."

"Oh! I don't want to get stung!" Flossie cried, as they went to a corner of the tent. There stood a three-foot model of the Honey Bunny float.

"It's bee-yoo-ti-ful!" Flossie exclaimed when she saw there were no live, buzzing insects.

On the back of the float was a bear standing on its hind legs. He was holding a honeycomb and looked as if he were going to devour it at any moment.

Squatting at the other end of the float was a large, white rabbit who stared at the bear.

"Just watch this," Timmy's father said. He

pressed a button and the bear raised the honeycomb to his mouth. But just as the bear stuck out a long, red tongue to taste the honey, a bee circled the bear's head. The bear lowered the honeycomb. His eyes rolled from side to side, following the bee.

The rabbit hopped forward one hop, and then back to its original position.

Freddie and Timmy jumped up and down, clapping their hands in excitement.

"That's neat!" Freddie said.

"Do it again, Daddy," Timmy begged.

As the bear, the bee, and the rabbit went through their motions again, Mr. Hamlin explained, "Each year the Tournament of Roses has a specific theme which all float entries must use in some way. This year the theme is 'Life Is Full of Surprises.' "

"The bee sure surprised the bear," Flossie giggled as Mary Cleary came over to the children.

"Part of the cocoon is dry now if you'd like to help us start putting the flowers on," she said.

"We're all ready," Nan replied, taking Flossie's hand.

As the painting team began applying the correct colors to one side of the float, volunteers started gluing the pretty blossoms to the other side.

One team was molding chicken wire into the shape of the huge Honey Bunny. Another was starting work on the enormous bear at the other end of the float.

Scaffolding was set up so workers could climb to the very top of both the rabbit and the bear to attach flowers to the ears.

"I want to put the flowers on the bee!" Freddie insisted.

"The bee hasn't been molded yet," Mary Cleary said, "but you can start to put yellow flowers on the big flatbed of the float."

"Okay," Freddie said without much enthusiasm. He watched closely as the young woman showed them how to glue the flowers onto the painted cocoon.

"What are all these tubes for?" Nan asked. She pointed to hundreds of small, glass tubes which were placed in the skin of the float.

"These are for the more fragile blossoms like the orchids and the roses," Miss Cleary explained. "They will be filled with water to make the flowers last longer. First we'll attach the heartier flowers like the mums and then apply the rest."

As the younger children glued flowers onto the bed of the float, Nan and Bert climbed the scaffolding to begin applying flowers to the back of the rabbit.

For almost an hour, everyone worked very hard. Then Nan happened to glance down.

"Oh, Bert—look!" she gasped.

Freddie, Flossie, and Timmy were throwing flowers at each other! The boys now began to glue blossoms to Flossie's face and arms!

"Stop that, you three!" Nan called.

Mr. Hamlin emerged from one end of the float. "Timothy Richard Hamlin!" he shouted sternly.

Instantly, the giggling children stood still, serious expressions on their faces.

Nan and Bert ran over to their younger brother and sister.

"You should be ashamed of yourself, Freddie," Bert said. "With all the flowers

that were ruined, how could you waste any?"

"And, Flossie—" Nan started to scold, but big tears began to fill Flossie's eyes.

"We didn't mean to do anything wrong," she said. "They were just making me look like Honey Bunny."

Mr. Hamlin walked over to his son. "Timothy, you know better than that!" he said. The boy and his friends looked so sad that the man's face softened a bit. "I know you didn't mean any harm," he added. "You were a big help decorating the float—until you started to decorate each other."

That evening the dinner table at the Hamlin house was unusually quiet. The younger children merely picked at their food. Nan, who was inclined to worry when anything went wrong, wondered what she could do to cheer them up.

Suddenly, she remembered the piñata and the mysterious message.

"Maybe we ought to think about ducks," Nan suggested.

"I forgot about that!" Freddie said.

"There are an awful lot of mysteries around here," Flossie commented.

Mrs. Hamlin smiled. "No more mysteries than Bobbsey twins," she said. "After you left this morning I discovered something else of interest."

"Really?" Bert asked.

Mrs. Hamlin excused herself briefly and returned with a wad of newspaper. Obviously, it had fallen out of the donkey piñata. The twins opened it immediately. Inside was a short, stubby pencil and some paper tied to it with a white string.

"What's it say?" Freddie asked.

Bert unfolded it quickly. The paper read:

ONCE THERE WAS A DUCK;
IT LAID AN EGG OF GOLD.
BY FOLLOWING THE FEATHER,
A TREASURE YOU'LL BEHOLD

"Ooh, a golden egg! A treasure!" Freddie cried. "Let's find it!"

"According to this message all we have to do is find a duck." Nan laughed.

"A duck, a duck. Where can we find a duck?" Flossie wondered.

"At the zoo!" Freddie shouted.

"Or the park," Timmy said.

"How about a pet shop?" Mr. Hamlin suggested.

"I think tomorrow's going to be a busy day," his wife added.

Bert suddenly snapped his fingers. "We really should search under the orange tree for more clues," he said.

"That's right," his twin chimed in. "After Flossie broke the piñata, we all left for the float factory. When we got back it was time to eat."

"Maybe we should start our investigation in the front yard," Freddie suggested. "After all, that's where the first clue popped up!"

"Good idea," Flossie said.

After being excused from the table, the young detectives scooted outside. They searched all around the orange tree, in the flower beds, and up and down the sidewalk but found no clues.

"I guess we'll just have to wait until we see a duck," Freddie said, disappointed.

"Just a minute," Timmy interrupted, pointing to the ground excitedly.

There in the grass lay a chubby green comb!

"It's a pick," Nan said. "The sort of thing used by people with very curly and very thick hair."

Bert tapped his fingers against his pants pocket. "Now, who do we know—" he mumbled.

"What about the kid you chased after the tent fell down?" Freddie said to his brother. "He had thick, curly hair."

"That's right," Nan agreed.

Everyone stared at each other anxiously. Was the troublemaker at the float factory lurking around the Hamlin house at that very moment?

·4·

Trapped!

Flossie shivered. "I'm scared," she said.

Nan hugged her younger sister. "Don't be afraid," she said. "Besides, how would the boy know where we're staying?"

"Maybe he overheard us talking before he made the tent fall," Freddie suggested.

"But it doesn't make sense for him to chance getting caught at the Hamlins' house," Bert observed.

Flossie giggled. "Maybe he's trying to send us on a wild duck chase."

"*May-be*," Nan agreed.

"And maybe not," Bert said. "I guess we won't know for sure until we find some more clues."

Next morning the children began their

search for the duck. First they went to a pet shop.

"Oh, look at the kittens!" Flossie cried gleefully. Two black-and-white kittens were playing with a tabby-colored one. They raced around the large cage, poking and chasing a small, blue ball.

Nan, meanwhile, spied a bright green parrot. "Good morning, Mr. Parrot," she greeted the bird.

"Good morning, good morning, good morning," the bird squawked back. Then he hopped down from his perch and began sticking his beak into the food at the bottom of the cage.

Freddie, Bert, and Timmy headed straight for the monkey in a castle-shaped cage. He bounced up and down, clapping his hands.

"Look! He's dancing!" Freddie exclaimed.

Almost at once, the monkey stopped. He pointed a hairy finger at the boys and covered his eyes with his other hand. Then he curled his upper lip and laughed loudly.

"Amos, stop that. You know it's not polite to make fun of people," said the store owner

who introduced himself as Mr. Dooby.

The monkey bowed his head contritely and walked to a small chair in the corner of the cage. He turned it away from his visitors and sat down.

"He's punishing himself for being bad," Timmy suggested.

"Oh, he's just pretending," the owner said. "Watch this." Mr. Dooby gave a sharp whistle. Instantly, the monkey popped out of the chair. He jumped up and down three times and turned somersaults all around the cage.

The boys cheered.

"What a talented monkey," Bert commented.

"Amos would also make somebody a great pet," the man said hopefully.

"Too bad we can't take him," Bert said sadly, "but we're just visiting Pasadena."

"Anyhow, we're really looking for a duck," Freddie piped up.

Seeing the man's puzzlement, Bert explained about the mystery.

"Hmmm," Mr. Dooby said. "Well, I'm afraid I can't help you. I haven't had any ducks in quite a while. But you might try the local park. It has a duck pond."

That was all the young detectives needed to hear. They asked for directions, thanked the man, and said good-bye to Amos.

The park was within walking distance, and when they reached it, they had no trouble finding the pond. There were several ducks waddling along the grassy edge. The others were in the water swimming in lazy circles. Timmy noticed one duck all by itself in the middle of the pond.

"Watch this," he said, opening a package of bread crumbs. He turned his back to the pond and flipped a handful over his shoulder. The crumbs sailed through the air and landed next to the duck. Immediately, it stretched out its long, gangly neck and gobbled them up before they sank in the water.

Freddie grinned at his friend. "Now it's my turn!" he said.

Flossie watched the two boys having fun together and she felt sad that Freddie seemed to prefer Timmy to her.

I can play too, she thought. She shut her eyes tightly and threw some crumbs as hard as she could. The bread flew high into the air, but landed on the grass by the pond.

Freddie and Timmy laughed. "Oh, Flossie, your bread didn't even get to the water," Freddie teased.

Flossie was ready to cry. She walked over to Nan and huddled close, while Bert, who had been scouting the area, came back.

"There's no golden egg buried around here. Let's go." He sighed impatiently.

"No, wait!" Nan said, having spied something. She pointed to a sign with an arrow. Printed above it were the words: TREASURE HUT—THIS WAY.

The young detectives quickly followed the winding path through clumps of trees and soon came to a small clearing. A large jungle gym and a sandbox stood in the middle.

"I bet the treasure is buried in the sandbox," Freddie said. Everyone hurried to it and began to dig.

"Oh, I've found something!" Flossie shouted. Excited, she scraped sand away from a round metal object. But her face dropped when she pulled out an old, rusty sand pail.

"Don't feel bad, Flossie," Nan said. "The rest of us didn't find anything at all. You found a pail at least."

Bert peered closely at the trees around the clearing. "Hey, everybody," he called out. "A log cabin."

The children darted to the small wooden house which was half hidden by the trees. A sign on the door said: TREASURE HUT!

"This is it!" Freddie exclaimed, as Bert led the way inside.

Nan's eyes immediately fell on an old iron box with a small rubber duck sitting on top of it!

"It looks like it's guarding something," Nan said.

"Maybe a rubber golden egg!" Flossie chirped.

Bert, Freddie, and Timmy carefully opened the lid which squeaked.

"It is GOLD!" Freddie exclaimed. His eyes opened wide.

Inside the box was a large sack filled with gold coins!

"That's a *real* treasure!" Flossie cried.

Bert reached into the sack and took one of the gold coins. He examined it briefly, then broke into a wide grin. He peeled off the gold paper and popped the coin into his mouth!

"Ummm, delicious." He laughed.

The others gulped.

"Bert, you're not supposed to eat money!" Flossie scolded.

"I'm not. It's candy."

"Huh?" Timmy asked

By now Freddie had also swallowed a piece. "It *is* candy!" he exclaimed. "This treasure is yummy—!"

The little boy had hardly spoken when the cabin door slammed shut! Before anyone could move, something large and heavy was dragged against it. *Thump!* It settled with a crash.

"Have fun!" a voice called playfully.

Bert ran to the door. He tried to push it open but couldn't.

"It's stuck!" he announced.

There was a cackling laugh outside, then the sound of someone running away.

The young detectives stared at each other. They were trapped!

·5·

Trouble Hut

Nan and Bert pushed against the door as hard as they could. It wouldn't budge at all!

"How about the window?" Flossie exclaimed, pointing to a very small opening near the ceiling.

"It's awfully small," Nan observed.

"Bet I could get through it," Timmy said.

Bert squatted quickly on all fours, allowing Timmy to climb on his shoulders. The boy tottered for a second, but with Nan's help, he kept his balance and Bert straightened up.

"There's a big tree right here!" Timmy exclaimed, peering through the dirty window. "All I have to do is climb out and down!"

He pushed against the window, but it

only moved up less than an inch.

"Push hard," Freddie told his friend.

"I am pushing hard, but it's stuck!" Timmy cried.

He dug his heels deep into Bert's shoulders and pressed forward on the window once more. This time it gave. The small boy crawled out, swinging one leg onto the thick limb, then the other.

"Hey, I see somebody on the other side of the clearing," Timmy reported. "I'm going to investigate."

"Open the door first!" Nan called out, but her words went unheard as the boy quickly scrambled away.

"Oh, Freddie, you should have gone instead," Flossie said. "Timmy's not a real detective like we are."

"Yes, he is. He found the comb under the orange tree, didn't he?"

"And he left us here, too!" Flossie answered back. She stepped crossly away from her brother. "I'll open the door myself."

"No, I'll go," Freddie said and with that, the older twins boosted him toward the window and he wriggled through.

Several minutes later he announced that a small seesaw was blocking the door!

"I can't move it. It's too heavy. Come help me, Floss," Freddie called though the Treasure Hut door.

As quickly as she could, Flossie wiggled through the window, too, and down the tree. Together, the young twins dragged the seesaw out of the way and Nan and Bert emerged.

"Where's Timmy?" Nan asked as she looked around.

"Timmy, where are you?" Freddie called.

There was no answer. Timmy Hamlin had disappeared!

"Maybe he was kidnapped!" Flossie exclaimed.

"I suggest we split up into two groups and start hunting for him," Bert said.

The boys headed down the path toward the duck pond while their sisters took the opposite direction. After an unsuccessful search, however, they all met back at the Treasure Hut.

"We'd better tell the police—" Nan started to say as Freddie interrupted her.

"Shh. Listen."

Someone was crying in the distance!

Very quietly, the Bobbseys moved in the direction of the sobbing sounds. Bert raised a finger to his lips and tiptoed to some bushes. He spread them apart and peered at the figure within. It *was* Timmy Hamlin!

"Timmy!" the older boy exclaimed. "What happened?"

"I twisted my ankle trying to chase the mystery person," he explained.

"Here, grab hold," Nan said, extending her arm.

With her on one side and Bert on the other, Timmy finally managed to stand up. Cautiously, he took a couple of steps.

"I can make it," he said.

"Did you see which direction the person went?" Bert asked.

Timmy nodded. "Through those trees. Right after I fell, I heard a roar like a motor starting up. It sounded like a small motorcycle."

"Or a moped?" Bert added.

"Maybe it was the same kid you saw at the float factory," Freddie said.

"I'd say we've got a lot of detective work ahead of us!" Bert remarked.

The twins helped Timmy walk to the bus stop where they caught the bus back to the Hamlin house. As they approached it, they noticed a police car in the driveway.

"I hope nothing's wrong," Nan said, gently restraining Timmy from running on his bad foot.

Inside they found a detective from the local police precinct. Mr. Hamlin was telling him all he knew about the vandalism at his float factory.

"I'm glad you got back before Lieutenant Edwards left," he said to the children. "The police have found a couple of clues. Look at this," he added, pointing to a piece of cloth on the coffee table.

"It's blue!" Bert exclaimed.

"Is something wrong?" Detective Edwards asked.

Quickly, Bert explained about the boy on the moped who was wearing a blue down vest.

"Very interesting," the detective said. "That description pretty much fits Raymond

Berry, the kid we caught shoplifting at Blumberger's Department Store."

"Where is he now? In jail?" Freddie asked in amazement.

The detective shook his head. "No. He's at his home over on Oakdale Drive. He and his mother live in the big, white house on the corner. The store didn't want to press charges since this was Raymond's first offense. The police only gave him a stiff warning."

Each of the twins knew what the others were thinking. They must go see Raymond and question him about the troublesome events at the Treasure Hut!

As Detective Edwards left the Hamlin house, he glanced at Bert with a twinkle in his eye. "You've really helped us a lot. Maybe someday you'll be a detective for real."

"We *are* real detectives," Freddie spoke up. "We've solved lots of mysteries!"

The policeman laughed. "In that case, I hope you can figure out this one," he said.

While Mrs. Hamlin bandaged Timmy's ankle, the Bobbseys decided to pay a visit to the Berry household. They found the address easily and Bert rang the doorbell.

"What do you want?" a thin woman demanded shortly, peering through the crack in the door.

"We'd like to talk with your son," Nan said politely.

"Ah, Ray—Raymond's in bed. He's, uh, he's not feeling good," the woman replied.

"It'll only take a minute," Bert said.

"He—ah—has a bad cold. You'll have to come back another time," the woman said.

Nan started forward. "But it's very important," she insisted.

"I think something funny is going on," Flossie whispered to her twin.

"I agree," Freddie whispered back. "She seems awfully nervous about something."

The woman hesitated a moment, then said, "Well, he's probably asleep. But I'll check." With that she walked through the living room and down a long hallway. She paused outside a closed door at the end of the hall.

The Bobbseys followed her.

"Raymond," Mrs. Berry called softly. "Are you awake?"

There was no answer.

The woman turned to the twins. "See, he's asleep, like I said."

Freddie bent down to tie his shoelace which had come undone. As he got up again, he leaned against the door to Raymond's room, causing it to swing open.

"Oh!" Mrs. Berry gasped, quickly pulling it shut. But the twin detective, had already glimpsed the perfectly made up bed. Raymond wasn't there!

·6·

Sticky Mysteries

"Where's Raymond?" Flossie asked Mrs. Berry.

"I thought you said he was sick in bed," Freddie added.

"Well, I forgot," the woman replied nervously. "He—he went to the drugstore for cough drops. He wanted to get them before going to bed." She half smiled at the twins, then pulled her head back stiffly. "Now tell me why you want to see my son."

Bert quickly told her about their disturbing adventure in the park.

"We think Raymond deliberately trapped us in the Treasure Hut," Nan said. She mentioned the accidents at the float factory and how her brother had chased the boy who rode a moped.

"Raymond wouldn't do any of those terrible things," Mrs. Berry insisted. "Believe me, you're completely mistaken. You know as well as I that there are probably fifty boys around here who look like him."

"But we—!" Nan started to say.

"No buts about it," the woman interrupted and ushered the children to the front door. "Good-bye."

On their way back to the Hamlin house, the twins discussed the situation.

"Even if Raymond didn't cause all the trouble, he always seems to be around when it happens," Bert observed. "I'd still like to talk to him."

"His mother sure doesn't want us to," Flossie said.

"Could be she's ashamed her son was caught shoplifting, and she's embarrassed to think Raymond is mixed up in other mischief," Nan suggested.

"Let's go back this evening and see him," Freddie said.

"That's a good idea," Bert agreed. "He

does have to come home sometime."

"Do you s'pose he really was out buying cough drops?" Flossie asked. "Maybe he was just causing more trouble."

"Who knows." Bert sighed as they turned the corner to the Hamlin house. "Race you to the front door, Floss."

The little girl ran as fast as she could, letting the breeze whip through her curls. Her brother was right behind. They raced up the driveway a few feet and came to an unexpected halt. Puzzled expressions crept over their faces!

"What's happening to my feet?" Flossie cried.

"And mine?" Bert asked.

Their shoes were stuck to the driveway!

Nan and Freddie had witnessed the scene and ran onto the grass to avoid getting caught also.

"What's the problem?" Nan inquired.

"Somebody poured glue all over the pavement," Bert said, lifting one foot, then the other.

"It's the same kind of stuff they use on the floats," Flossie observed. "It's not shiny like

most glue and it's extra sticky."

She started to wiggle her feet, freeing both shoes and Bert quickly scooped her up and carried her to the grass.

"Now who would make such a mess?" Flossie asked.

"Who do you think?" Freddie replied.

"Raymond?"

"Who else?"

"Well, this is something else to ask him about," Bert said. "Meantime we'd better tell Mrs. Hamlin so she can warn Mr. Hamlin before he drives home."

He and Flossie walked around to the back porch and left their shoes there, while Nan and Freddie went in the front way.

Finding Mrs. Hamlin in the kitchen, they told her what had just occurred.

"How awful!" she said, staring at the two shoeless children. "Are you all right?"

"I'm fine." Flossie giggled. "It just felt funny to be stuck to the driveway."

"Did you see anyone strange hanging around the house?" Bert asked Timmy's mother.

"No, but I wasn't here all afternoon. I went next door to see Mrs. Mead for a little while. She just came home from the hospital." Mrs. Hamlin paused before adding, "Perhaps Timmy saw someone, though. He's been in his room and it overlooks the driveway."

The twins hurried upstairs to discover the young boy sitting up in bed with his bandaged ankle propped on a pillow. The children quickly explained what had happened.

"I saw him!" Timmy said excitedly. "He spilled something on our driveway. I thought it was soda."

"So you saw Raymond do it?" Freddie declared.

Timmy shook his head. "It wasn't Raymond," he replied. "This boy didn't have curly, blond hair. It was dark and straight."

The twins looked at each other, puzzled.

"Are you sure?" Freddie asked.

"Sure I'm sure."

"Then there are two mischief-makers!" Flossie concluded.

"Maybe they're friends," Nan said, and Timmy went on.

"If I had known he was pouring glue, I would've chased him."

"With that bad ankle of yours, it's just as well you didn't," Bert replied. "Anyhow, if you hadn't seen the dark-haired boy, we would've accused Raymond by mistake. Then we'd all be in trouble."

"Even so," Timmy moaned, "I wish I were a better detective."

As he slid down against the headboard, letting his features set in a frown, Mrs. Hamlin stepped into the room. She was holding two envelopes.

"I just checked the mail and found these. They're addressed to the Bobbsey twins," she said.

"Maybe one is from Mommy and Daddy," Flossie said happily.

Bert and Nan opened the envelopes. Inside Bert's was a torn piece of paper that said:

BOBBSEYS—STICK TO YOUR OWN BUSINESS!

Flossie's eyes grew wide. "What does yours say, Nan?" she asked anxiously.

Her sister pulled out a plain white card. On it was printed the following:

YOU FOUND ONE TREASURE—
HOORAY FOR YOU!
AROUND THE CORNER ANOTHER ONE WAITS.
CAN YOU FIND IT TOO?

"The notes were obviously written by two different people," Bert said.

"Yours must have been written by the person who caused all the damage at the float factory!" Freddie told his brother.

"But who wrote the other note?" Flossie asked. "And what does it mean?"

·7·

Freddie's Close
Call

Nan studied the intriguing message on the white card. "So another treasure is around the corner. Well, there's only one way to find out what it is." She dashed out of the room and down the stairs.

"Hey, wait for me!" Freddie exclaimed, trailing after her.

"We'll come, too," Bert called after them. "Flossie and I just have to put on shoes."

But Timmy begged the two children to stay. "Don't you want to play a game or something?" he asked limply.

Flossie curled her lips. "I guess so," she said, even though she and her brother would have preferred to hunt for treasure.

"It must be boring to sit alone in your room all afternoon," Bert added and dug through a chest of toys and games.

Nan and Freddie, meanwhile, were carefully scouring the Hamlins' yard. They were so intent on their search that they didn't even notice the other twins had remained in the house.

"I don't see anything that looks like a treasure," Nan said.

"Maybe it's hidden inside something else," the little boy replied. "Like up in that palm tree." He ran to it and peered up into the feathery branches.

"No treasure here," he said shortly.

"Maybe it's hidden underneath the shrubbery," Nan suggested. They got down on their hands and knees and began to poke through the bushes. Before they were done, however, Freddie suddenly excused himself.

"I've got an idea," he cried and raced off, leaving his sister to finish the job.

"Freddie," she called a few minutes later. "Freddie, where are you?"

There was no reply.

That's strange, Nan thought.

She glanced around the front yard, but the young detective was nowhere in sight. She checked the palm tree and the orange tree but he wasn't in either of them. She circled around to the back of the house and peeked into the garage, but it was empty too. Where had he gone?

Then she heard her name. It was Freddie calling. His voice seemed far away, though, as if it were coming from the sky. Nan craned her neck and stepped back a few paces. She barely glimpsed her brother's head above the garage roof!

"Freddie! What are you doing up there? Get down right this minute!" Nan demanded.

But Freddie ignored his sister's order. "I've got something to show you," he said instead. "Come on up."

"Well, that does it. I guess I'll have to go up and get you," Nan muttered.

She hurried into the garage where she spied a makeshift ladder leading to a small attic. Nan climbed quickly and discovered a window that opened onto the gently sloping roof.

Cautiously, the dark-haired girl crept outside. Her eyes darted in every direction for Freddie. He had disappeared again. Had he fallen? she wondered fearfully.

"Freddie?" she called.

"Over here, Nan." The boy's voice drifted in from the back of the roof.

"Freddie—be careful!" she warned, moving slowly toward him.

"But I see something!" the boy detective exclaimed. "I think it's the treasure!"

In his excitement, the young twin jumped up and down on his toes.

"Oh, Fre—" Nan half cried as he tottered off balance.

She hurried forward, trying to catch him, but it was too late! His feet flew out from under him and he fell against the sloping roof with a crash!

"Oh, Nan! I'm sliding!" Freddie shrieked. He was only a few feet away from the edge.

"Grab onto the roof!" his sister urged.

"Spread your hands out and press down hard!"

Small drops of perspiration glistened on his nose as he obeyed. Almost instantly, he stopped moving. But then he tried to stand up and his feet slipped again.

"*Help!*" he shouted.

Nan dived for his outstretched arm, holding it tightly and glimpsing the ground below at the same time. For a second, she felt dizzy.

I can't fall, she told herself.

"My foot's caught in something!" Freddie cried.

"Stay still," Nan answered. "You're probably stuck in the rain gutter."

She crawled closer and clasped Freddie's other hand, pulling him toward her. As she did, the gutter ripped away from the roof and the boy's foot yanked free, dangling in space!

"I'm going to fall, I'm going to fall!" Freddie whimpered.

"No, you're not," his sister said. "Just take it slow and easy."

Her hands were cold and clammy like his, but she kept her grip steady, helping the twin edge himself upward.

"Oh, Freddie," Nan said, gulping back tears when he was safely next to her, "if I hadn't caught you, you would have planted yourself in Mrs. Hamlin's garden."

"I know," Freddie said. He was still shaking but not ready to climb down yet.

"That's what I wanted you to see—the garden!" he explained. Nan hung onto him as he pointed to a patch of vegetables growing on a long vine.

"I don't see anything," she replied.

"There—right there!" Freddie persisted, waving his chubby fingers.

The girl fixed her eyes squarely on a bushy plant. Growing out of a large, leafy stalk were several dollar bills.

"I don't believe it!" Nan gasped in amazement.

"It's a real live money tree!" Freddie exclaimed.

The twins immediately crawled back to the roof window, through the attic, and down the steps. They all raced around the garage to the garden behind it. Sure enough, money was stuck to the leaves of not one but three plants!

"I told you—it's the treasure!" Freddie declared gleefully.

"I wonder how it got here," Nan said.

"I don't know, but now I'm glad I climbed to the roof. I figured I could see everywhere then."

"Wait till we show Bert and Flossie," Nan remarked, harvesting the money from the plants.

"And what about Mr. and Mrs. Hamlin?" Freddie giggled as he peeled off a few dollar bills too. "They must've used some very special plant seeds."

Nan rolled her eyes at the little boy. "Everybody knows money doesn't grow on trees." She grinned.

Before Freddie could answer, however, a voice cut in from behind them. "Hey, you! That belongs to me!"

The twin detectives whirled around quickly and were greeted by a big blast of water in their faces!

·8·

Raymond's Tumble

Nan and Freddie were blinded by the burst of water from the Hamlins' garden hose. They sputtered and coughed as they turned away from the powerful stream, trying to catch their breath.

Blinking through little drops of water on their eyelids, they saw a black-haired boy holding the hose! He threw it to the ground and began to grab some of the dollar bills from the plants.

"Stop that!" Nan cried. She ran over to the boy but he moved sharply aside.

He clutched a few more dollar bills and then sped down the yard next to the drive-way without looking behind him.

"Come back here!" Freddie shouted, racing after the boy as fast as he could.

By now, Bert and Flossie had heard the commotion. They flew out of the Hamlin house and joined the chase. The other twins were several feet ahead, running hard too. But the mysterious boy had cut through a neighboring yard into a vacant lot.

"I bet he's the kid who spilled glue all over the driveway," Bert said to Nan when he finally caught up to her.

"You could be right," Nan panted.

The boy charged rapidly toward a low fence overgrown with tall grass and weeds.

"If he gets over that fence, he'll escape!" Nan cried. She put on an extra burst of speed.

Only a step away from the fence, the boy looked back fearfully to see where the twins were. He jumped into the air and disappeared over the other side.

Swiftly, Nan and Bert reached the fence. Bert vaulted it easily and Nan scrambled over the middle railing. They looked all around but the boy had completely disappeared!

The younger twins reached the fence and wiggled through it.

"Where did he go?" Freddie asked, turning in all directions.

"He just vanished," his older sister replied.

"I think we ought to split up and look for any clues he might have accidentally left behind," Bert suggested.

"Good idea," Flossie agreed.

Each twin then began to walk slowly in a

different direction, searching the ground carefully for anything which might tell them more about the dark-haired mischief-maker.

Freddie followed a winding path to the other side of the vacant lot. When he reached the far side, he noticed a thick hedge that almost covered the path. Suddenly, he spied something white caught on one of the lower branches.

Eagerly, he reached for it and discovered it was a small, folded envelope. On the front of it was written:

RAYMOND BERRY
172 OAKDALE DRIVE
PASADENA, CALIFORNIA

"Over here!" Freddie shouted to the others. "I've found a clue!"

Everyone crowded around the young boy as he showed them his discovery.

"What's inside?" Flossie asked. "Open it, Freddie."

Her twin brother pulled at the flap and drew out a photograph of a man and woman standing by a sailboat. Inside the boat was a thin, curly-haired boy. He was waving at the camera and smiling broadly.

"That looks like the kid I chased out of the float factory!" Bert exclaimed. "I bet it's Raymond."

"And that looks like Raymond's mother," Nan added.

"Only she seems very happy in this picture," Flossie observed.

"Do you suppose that's Raymond's father?" Freddie said.

"Probably," Bert answered. "But I'm wondering how the dark-haired boy got hold of this envelope."

"Maybe he stole it," Nan said. "At least, we can return it to Raymond this evening when we go to his house. It's a great excuse to try seeing him again."

Bert nodded in agreement, while his younger brother peered into the envelope once more.

"Find something?" Flossie asked eagerly.

"Uh-huh. Look!"

The little boy eagerly pulled out a newspaper clipping that had been folded into a tiny square and opened it. The headline said: LOCAL MAN DIES IN CAR CRASH.

"Oh, how terrible!" Nan exclaimed, quickly reading the story. "Mr. Berry was killed in an automobile accident only a few months ago."

"Maybe that's why Raymond has been getting into so much trouble," Bert remarked.

Although the young detectives were tempted to go straight to the Berrys' house, they realized it was almost time for supper so they went back to the Hamlins' instead.

When they reached the house, however, they discovered the family sitting in the living room. They all had very serious expressions on their faces.

"Here, Bert," Mr. Hamlin said, handing the boy a piece of paper.

"More trouble?" Bert replied. He read the message out loud. "It says: 'BEWARE! BEWARE! YOUR FLOATS WILL NEVER LAST UNTIL THE PARADE!' "

"When did this come?" Nan inquired.

"It was in the mailbox along with the other notes for you," Mrs. Hamlin replied.

"The handwriting is the same as the one on the warning we got," the girl said.

"You're right," Freddie said. "But who sent it?"

"I don't know," Mr. Hamlin replied, "but it might very well be the same person who's been making threatening phone calls to the factory."

"What are we going to do?" Mrs. Hamlin asked anxiously.

"Since the parade is tomorrow we only have to worry about tonight," her husband said. "It will be practically impossible for anyone to get past the float decorators. But just to be on the safe side, I think I'll spend the night at the factory. I have to be up at three anyway."

"In the morning?" Nan gasped.

The man grinned. "That's when the final judging is," he told her. "Awards will be given to some of the floats—awards for originality, most beautiful entry, best use of roses, and so forth."

"Do you think Honey Bunny will win a prize?" Flossie asked.

"We sure hope so," Mrs. Hamlin replied, "but there's always a lot of competition so we're not counting on it."

"Oh, Daddy, can't we go with you?" Timmy begged. "We could sleep out in the tents and help guard the floats!"

His parents stared at each other.

"We could pitch the tents in the back of the factory next to the fence by the trees. Then we wouldn't be in anybody's way and we could guard the back gate at the same time. *Please!*" the boy implored.

"I suppose it would be okay," his mother said slowly. "So long as your father agrees."

Mr. Hamlin nodded. "It might be fun for them," he said to his wife, "and who knows, they might be able to help with some of the last-minute work."

"Yippee!" the children exclaimed.

"In that case, we'll have to wait until tomorrow to give Raymond his envelope," Nan said and quickly related the twins' adventure involving the mysterious boy.

"I suggest you leave the envelope and photograph here," Timmy's mother advised. "That way it won't get lost. You can take it to the Berrys' house after the parade."

"Better pack your bags now," Mr. Hamlin said. "You'll need a change of clothing for tomorrow. We've got a lot of work to do tonight."

The twins hurried to their rooms wondering about the adventure ahead. Would they come face to face with the person who had sent the threatening warnings?

·9·

At the Float Factory

The young detectives talked excitedly about the mysterious threats as Mr. Hamlin drove toward the float factory.

"What if the person who's been making them really does show up and he's six feet tall?" Freddie asked the other children.

"We'll just have to stand on top of each other and face him eyeball to eyeball!" Nan giggled.

"That's bound to scare him off!" Mr. Hamlin grinned.

By the time they pulled into the parking lot, the conversation had shifted to plans for supper. To the twins' delight, Mary Cleary greeted them with an armload of hot dog buns.

"Hope you all have big appetites!" she said.

"Boy, do we!" Bert exclaimed.

"They're going to help us decorate," Mr. Hamlin told the young woman, "so we'd better feed them double of everything!"

"Do you always have a cookout?" Nan asked.

"Sure do, especially since we can't go to a New Year's Eve party," Mary Cleary said. "We usually end up working all night long to get the floats ready for the parade the next day."

Several feet beyond the group, two workers had started to grill hot dogs and hamburgers. Nan and Bert offered to help while the younger twins and Timmy went to pitch tents in the yard behind the factory.

"Come and get it!" Mr. Hamlin called out before long, drawing everybody to the barbecue.

When they had finished eating, he raised his hand for silence and explained about the threatening note and phone calls.

"I don't want to worry you," he concluded, "but we all have to keep particularly alert tonight. If you notice anything suspicious, report it immediately. Now we've got some floats to build." He grinned. "Back to work!"

The Bobbsey twins and Timmy raced to their chores. They didn't stop once until Mr. Hamlin caught Freddie and Flossie yawning.

"Time for bed, I guess," the man said, and the younger children nodded.

The older twins, however, worked until just after eleven o'clock. Reluctantly, they left the final touches to the other workers and walked sleepily to their tents.

"I hope everything will be okay," Nan said.

"With so many people around, I don't see how anyone could damage the floats," Bert replied. "See you in the morning."

Nan nodded as she crawled into the space she was sharing with Flossie while Bert checked on Freddie and Timmy. Then the older boy slipped into his sleeping bag. He listened to the sounds coming from the float factory. This sure has been a fun vacation, he thought. Who ever would have believed we'd get to help build a float for the Rose Parade?

Suddenly, he heard a different sound. It was nearby but very soft. He listened intently for a moment. It sounded like metal scraping against metal. Was it the chain link fence behind the tents?

Bert sat up and shook his younger brother. "Freddie. Freddie. Wake up," he whispered urgently.

"Wha-what's that?" Freddie asked sleepily.

"I don't know!" Bert said.

Again the soft, scraping sound came.

"Let's investigate," Freddie suggested.

"I'm coming too," put in Timmy who had awakened.

But before the younger boys could crawl out of their sleeping bags, something large stumbled against the side of their tent causing it to sway. The wall held only for a moment, then crashed down on top of Freddie and Timmy.

"Help!" the two boys shrieked while Bert pushed the canvas off them.

The noise brought Nan and Flossie running out of their tent, and soon Bert and the other boys were free of theirs as well. They saw someone dart into the shadows of the float factory.

"It's the dark-haired boy!" Nan exclaimed.

"Let's get him!" Bert shouted, dashing forward.

But the boy ducked quickly behind some equipment stored next to the building and disappeared.

"You take one side," Bert told his twin, "and I'll take the other."

Nan raced to the far side of the equipment and then began to creep back toward her brother. Suddenly, something moved in the shadows!

"It's him!" Nan gasped.

He was looking over his shoulder to see if anyone was following him and bolted right into the girl! Both of them fell, and Nan held onto his arm tightly.

"Ouch!" he hollered. He twisted and struggled to get away, but the others had already surrounded him.

"Get up! Now!" Bert ordered, grabbing

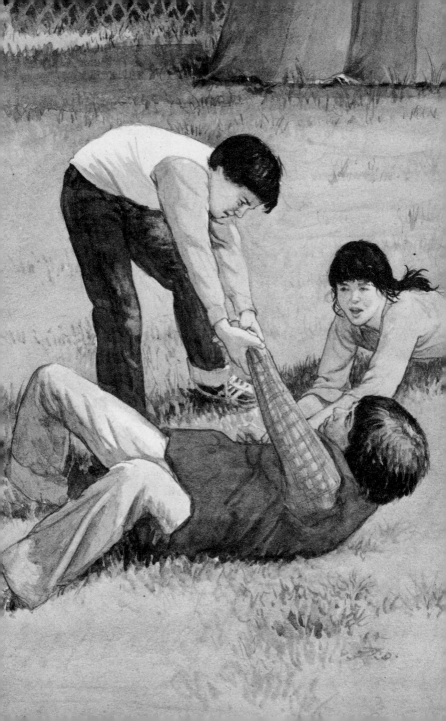

the boy and pulling him to his feet.

"Let go of me!" the young captive bellowed.

"Not yet," Bert replied. "You have a lot of explaining to do!"

The boy grunted something and tried to break free. He kicked at the children but stumbled. That was when Freddie noticed a few strands of curly, blond hair peeking under an elasticized band.

"You're wearing a wig!" the little detective announced and pulled it off.

"Raymond!" everyone chorused.

"How do you know my name?"

Just then, Mr. Hamlin and Mary Cleary appeared in the doorway of the factory.

"We thought we heard something," the young woman said.

"What's going on out there?" Timmy's father demanded. "All of you come over here right this minute!"

"We caught our suspect!" Timmy declared proudly.

"And look what he was carrying," Bert added, picking up a heavy metal bucket from the ground.

"It's tar!" Mary Cleary exclaimed as she and Mr. Hamlin stepped toward the group. "Where did you get this?" she asked Raymond.

"Down the road," the boy said sullenly. He pointed in the direction of a road repair team.

"And how did you get in here?" Mr. Hamlin said sternly.

"Through the fence."

A quick examination revealed that some of the bottom sections of the chain link fence had been cut enough to allow the bucket to be pushed inside. Raymond had crawled in after it.

"I am taking you home," Mr. Hamlin informed the boy abruptly. "We still have a lot to do on the floats so I'll deal with you in the morning. Come on."

"May I ask a question first?" Nan interrupted. "Raymond, were you the person who sent all of those terrible notes?"

"And locked us in the Treasure Hut?" Freddie exclaimed.

"I don't know what you're talking about," Raymond insisted.

"But I saw you running away in the park," Timmy said.

Raymond did not answer.

"Look, son, you're in a lot of trouble over what happened here tonight. Timmy says he saw you. So did Bert—after you tried to destroy the flowers in my tent," Mr. Hamlin put in. "Lying won't help matters."

Raymond lowered his head.

"So you admit to the pranks?" the man continued.

Before Raymond could answer, Nan suddenly reached into her back pocket and pulled out a bright green comb. "And is this yours?" she asked.

Raymond nodded slowly. "I just didn't want you guys messing around in my business. I was keeping an eye on you."

"Well, we'll have to straighten everything out tomorrow," Mr. Hamlin said, leading the boy to his car. "It's very late now and I'm sure your mother is worried about you."

As they pulled out of the parking lot, the twins and Timmy fixed the fallen tent.

"At least we know the floats will be safe," Flossie remarked shortly.

"True, but we still don't know who put the treasure in the Treasure Hut or who planted the money tree," Nan said.

"We'll just have to do some more detective work after the parade," Bert said, gulping back a yawn. "Right now, we'd better all get some sleep."

The rest of the night passed uneventfully and in the morning Mrs. Hamlin picked up the children for breakfast at a nearby pancake house. Then they drove to the float lineup at Wrigley Gardens.

"I didn't even hear the floats leave," Freddie said.

"Me neither," Flossie added out of Nan's earshot.

She was gazing at the large, stately mansion surrounded by a gracious lawn and many kinds of roses.

"What a beautiful place," she said.

"That's called Tournament House," Mrs. Hamlin explained. "It was once the home of William Wrigley, Junior, the famous chewing gum manufacturer. Now it's the headquarters for the Tournament of Roses Association."

The sound of over twenty marching bands tuning up and practicing filled the air. The colorful costumes of their members added to the excitement as tardy players dashed to their places.

Horses in equestrian units snorted and stamped their hooves. All were draped in lavish silver trappings that glittered in the early morning sun.

"Look at that lady," Bert said as a rider on horseback passed in front of the twins. She wore an elegant, gold satin gown and a sleek, black cape with gold trim.

"The equestrians have been an important part of the Rose Parade since its beginning in 1890," Mrs. Hamlin informed the children.

"How many floats are there altogether?" Bert asked as they moved toward the front of the lineup.

"Sixty in all."

Now they spotted the Honey Bunny float and Mr. Hamlin. He saw them too and darted forward. There was an enormous grin on his face.

"We won the Judges' Special Award for Best Display of Humor!" he exclaimed.

"We did?" his wife said excitedly. "How wonderful!"

"Hooray for Honey Bunny!" the twins cheered, while Timmy slipped under his father's arm for an affectionate pat.

"Mr. Hamlin," Freddie asked, "how come nobody's on your float? All the others have people."

"You kids sure notice everything," the man replied with a soft chuckle. "That's the surprise I promised you. How would you all like to ride in the parade?"

"On the Honey Bunny float?" Timmy replied.

"Of course."

"Oh, sir—" Bert gasped.

"But we don't have any costumes," Nan pointed out.

"Yes, you do," a voice interrupted. It was Mary Cleary. She was holding a large cardboard box which she opened rapidly.

"A bunny! I'm a little bunny!" Flossie laughed when Mary handed her a costume.

"Hey, Freddie. We're both carrots!" Timmy giggled.

Freddie turned to his twin. "I know one bunny who'd better not try eating this carrot," he smirked.

Nan was to be a head of lettuce and her brother Bert took the bear cub costume. He slipped into the outfit promptly and practiced waving his paws in the air and growling in a deep, husky voice.

"Oh, Bert, you don't scare me at all," Flossie said nonchalantly.

When all the costumes had been distributed, Mary Cleary noticed something lying in the bottom of the box. "What's this?" she asked, picking up a white envelope. "I'm sure it wasn't there last night when I packed the costumes."

The mystery letter was addressed to THE BOBBSEY TWINS.

· 10 ·

A Rosy Finale

Nan, who was standing by the float worker, took the envelope and opened it. Tucked inside was a small piece of paper and on it were the words:

THE BOBBSEY TWINS ARE THE GREATEST!

More intriguing to the young detectives was what was taped underneath. It was a duck feather!

Mr. Hamlin laughed. "Well, we know one float is certainly living up to the theme of this year's parade: 'Life Is Full of Surprises.'"

"This message is another clue," Flossie declared, "but what does it mean?"

"You'll have plenty of time to think about it," Mrs. Hamlin said. "The parade route is five and a half miles long."

"That's not so long," Freddie said.

"It is when you're creeping at a snail's pace," the woman replied. "It takes about two hours to get from one end to the other."

"Too bad Mom and Dad won't be able to see us," Nan said wistfully.

"How do you know they won't?" Bert replied. "They'll probably be watching the parade on television in Hawaii. You know Dad always likes to see Mr. Hamlin's floats."

He carefully pocketed the envelope with the note and the duck feather as a nervous young man in a white suit hurried up to them.

"Mr. Hamlin," the fellow said, consulting a clipboard, "you only have eight minutes to get ready. The Grand Marshal's car with Miss Amy Potter just took off and the Mayor's car is right behind hers."

"Okay, Terry, we're set to roll," Mr. Hamlin said calmly.

He helped the twins, Timmy, and Mary Cleary up onto the float and showed them where to stand. "Just smile and wave to the crowds," he said. "We'll meet you at Victory Park where all the floats are left on display after the parade."

"Stay on the float until we get there," Mrs. Hamlin added. "The park will be swarming with people and we don't want to lose you!"

The couple said good-bye to the children and walked back to their car hand in hand.

Before anyone had time to become nervous, the man with the clipboard came up to the float. "Honey Bunny float, are you ready?" he asked.

"Yes," everyone said.

"Oh, come on. You can do better than that. You don't sound very excited about being in the parade. Let's try it again." He flashed a big smile. "Honey Bunny float, are you ready?"

This time everyone laughed and sang out, "Y-y-e-e-s-s-s!"

"Then, Honey Bunny float, please join our parade," he said and tapped his clipboard against the float three times.

The float began to inch foward! Ever so

slowly, the mechanical bunny took a small hop forward and then jumped back. The big, brown bear brought the honeycomb to his mouth and stuck out his red tongue to taste it. Then the bee circled his head and the bear's eyes followed the buzzing insect.

People on other floats pointed to the Honey Bunny float and applauded.

"How does the float move?" Freddie asked Mary Cleary who was standing beside him.

"The frame is mounted on a car or a tractor. A man drives it while looking through small holes in the front of the float," she replied.

"It must be very hard to see where he's going," Freddie said.

"It is. But there's a pink line painted down the center of the street and that's a big help. All the driver has to do is follow it to the end of the parade," the young woman added.

As the Honey Bunny float traveled down Colorado Boulevard, people all along the route laughed at the antics of the bear and the bee. They clapped as Honey Bunny

hopped back and forth. The riders all waved and smiled proudly.

Finally, the float turned onto Sierra Madre Boulevard for the final stretch of the parade. A block before Victory Park, it passed the second of two official press and photography stands.

Suddenly, Nan gasped in amazement. "Look in the stands—in the first row. It's Mom and Dad!"

"They're back!" Freddie shouted as Mr. Bobbsey snapped a picture of the float. Mrs. Bobbsey waved a white handkerchief and blew a big kiss to the riders.

"Hooray!" Flossie cried.

Bert let out his loudest bear cub roar.

"Oh, Bert, why are you trying to scare Mommy like that?" Flossie said.

Her older brother just laughed. He knew it wouldn't be long before the Bobbsey family was reunited again. When the float finally pulled to a halt several minutes later, the twins spotted their parents in the onrush of people. Mr. and Mrs. Hamlin also emerged from the visitors' center, and with them was a pleasant-looking woman.

"Who's that?" Flossie asked Timmy.

"Miss Amy Potter. She's the Grand Marshal of the Rose Parade."

"Ooh—the famous author," the little girl said, duly impressed.

"She's a friend of my mother's," Timmy added. "They went to school together."

As the little boy spoke, Mr. and Mrs. Bobbsey joined the group which by now included the Hamlins and Miss Potter. All the Bobbseys hugged each other in happy reunion.

"Thank you for my train set," Timmy said to the author.

"Yeah, it's great!" Freddie piped up.

Flossie merely kicked the grass with one shoe. "I'm hungry," she murmured but no one except Miss Potter heard her.

"May I please have your autograph?" Bert asked, his voice rising over Flossie's. "I've read so many of your books. I wish I had one with me for you to sign."

"Well, I'm sure I have a piece of paper in my purse," the woman replied. Then, glancing at Flossie, she added with a smile, "I have a little something for you, too."

Miss Potter opened her purse and rummaged through the contents quickly. Bert grinned as she pulled out a pad and wrote her name, then handed his younger sister a piece of candy.

The other twins gaped in astonishment! It was a gold-foiled chocolate!

"From the Treasure Hut!" Flossie exclaimed.

Bert now produced the note that was in the costume box and compared the handwriting with Miss Potter's signature. They were the same!

"Did you plant the money tree, too?" Freddie asked.

"Yes," the author admitted sheepishly.

"So Mrs. Hamlin's hunch was right," Freddie said in awe. "We did solve the duck mystery today!"

"I really ought to explain." Timmy's mother laughed. "When I told Miss Potter that four young detectives were coming to visit us, she said, 'Let's cook up a little mystery for them to solve just for fun!' "

Timmy Hamlin's eyes popped wide. "So you were part of the whole thing, Mommy!" he exclaimed.

His mother nodded. "I guess you could call me an accomplice of sorts," she replied. "Of course, at the time we thought up the mystery, we had no idea you'd have to solve a real one, too!"

"The more the better!" Nan exclaimed. "Life really is full of mysteries, but the best one is that Mom and Dad returned early."

"Thank you, dear," Mrs. Bobbsey said, hugging her daughter. "Mr. Hamlin phoned us in Hawaii to say that the children who were supposed to ride on the Honey Bunny float wouldn't be able to. He asked if you could take their places."

"We were lucky to catch an earlier flight back," Mr. Bobbsey said.

"I'm glad you did," Bert said.

"Me, too!" Freddie and Flossie chimed in.

Nan, in the meantime, had caught sight of Raymond's mother standing next to one of the floats. "Do you have Raymond's envelope with you?" she asked Mrs. Hamlin.

Nan nodded in the other woman's direction.
"Indeed I do."

She and Nan, followed by Mrs. Bobbsey,
walked toward Mrs. Berry. As quickly as she
could, Nan explained how the twins had
found the envelope and gave it to her.

"Oh, thank you," the woman said. "Raymond has been very upset since he discovered he had lost it. You see, this was the last
photograph taken of Raymond's father before he was in that awful car accident." Tears
sprang to her eyes.

Mrs. Hamlin softly pressed the woman's
hand in sympathy.

"I want to apologize for all the trouble my
son has been causing," Mrs. Berry continued, "and for my behavior the other day.
Raymond and his father were very close and
I'm afraid Raymond still isn't over the shock
of losing him. Money has been tight for us
too."

She swallowed hard before going on.

"It's not necessary to tell us any more,"
Mrs. Hamlin said.

"Oh, but I want to. Raymond knew that
one of the float factories had promised me a

job if they got certain contracts for this year's parade. A couple of them went to your husband, though, and Raymond mistakenly blamed your husband for the fact I couldn't get a job with the other factory."

"Are you still looking for work?" Mrs. Hamlin asked instantly.

"Yes, I am."

Mrs. Bobbsey and Nan smiled at each other, as Timmy's mother continued.

"Well, if you're interested, I could speak to my husband about a position in his office. He told me that one of his employees is moving back East next month."

"Are you sure? I mean, that sounds wonderful," Mrs. Berry replied happily. "Oh, how can I ever thank you?"

Excited, Nan ran back to the others and told them all that Mrs. Berry had said.

Amy Potter's eyes twinkled as the girl finished speaking. "Now that you've solved all the mysteries here, what are you going to do next?" she asked.

The older twins shrugged while Freddie whispered to Flossie. "Want to play trains when we get home?"

"Oh, *yes*," she said, dimpling her cheeks in a deep grin.

"How about helping me on my new book as well?" the author went on.

"What's it about?" Nan inquired eagerly.

"An ancient jeweled necklace that was stolen from a famous actress."

"Who stole it?" Flossie inquired.

"That's the problem. No one seems to know."

Completely intrigued, Bert said, "We'd love to help you, Miss Potter, but we'll have to wait until our next school vacation."

None of the Bobbsey twins expected to become immediately involved in *The Camp Fire Mystery* when they returned home to Lakeport.

"In the meantime," Amy Potter said, "I'll try to piece a few clues together on my own. But don't forget I'm counting on you to figure out the solution. After all, the Bobbsey twins are the greatest!"

THE BOBBSEY TWINS® SERIES
by Laura Lee Hope